In Love with my Best Friend

TROUBLED GIRLS FIND LOVE

KATHRYN REIGN

KATHRYN REIGN PUBLISHING

Copyright

In Love with my Best Friend

Cover Design by Les (germancreative)

In Love with my Best Friend

In Love with my Best Friend
Blurb

My name is Lauren.

I have a caring husband and two beautiful children.

But I can't stop thinking about... **Him**.

Ever since I found my old phone, I've been haunted by memories of Felix, bringing back feelings that I've tried so hard to ignore.

I feel guilty for regretting my marriage, for channeling the affection I should be having for my husband onto another man.

But I can no longer deny it.

I'm in love with my best friend.

A romance short story that features love, regret, and betrayal.

Contents

Chapter One

I wake up in my bedroom, staring up at the plain, white ceiling. Letting out a small sigh, I climb out of my comfy bed and head downstairs, my ears suddenly being greeted by the sound of my children.

"Good morning!" My husband gives me a small smile when I enter the living room. He's sitting on the couch, the children playing in front of him. "I have to work today. But I'll try to come home early and spend the evening with you."

Nodding, I take a seat beside him, looking down at our children playing on the carpet. We have a three-year-old boy and a two-year-old girl, both of them beautiful children and look exactly like my husband. I kneel in front of my son, his small face coming toward me.

"Look, Mommy! I got a new car!" He shows me his toy, his face lighting up as he speaks about it.

I giggle as I take the toy from him. "Wow! Did your father get this for you?" I look over at my husband, who's beaming at us.

"We bought it from the toy store yesterday..." He stands up and starts to head toward the front door, fixing his tie on the way. "I'm heading to work now... Also, I found your old phone in the attic. I'm not sure if you want to look at it or not. It's on the kitchen counter."

Getting back onto my feet, I go to see my husband off, shutting the door tightly behind him. I think to myself for a moment... Do I really want to look at that phone? I know it will only bring back memories that I had worked so hard to bury.

However, I can't bring myself to ignore my feelings any longer. I rush into the kitchen, spotting the phone on the side of the counter.

As I pick it up, the memories of my past life all flood back to me. All of my friends... Him. I feel a shiver run down my spine as I remember the sound of his voice, and the feeling of his fingers against my skin. Mentally scolding myself for even thinking such things about another man, I click the on button. As I expected, it's dead. I search through the kitchen drawers, desperately trying to find a charger that will be able to fit the phone.

It doesn't take me long to find something, and I plug it in, my heart beating quickly. I don't know what I will find on here. I don't even know if everything will be as I left it. As I ponder, I see the icon that signals that the phone is turning on, and then the lock screen. The picture is of Felix, my best friend at the time, and the only one I had ever felt strongly toward.

As I stare at his face, my heart begins to drop. All this time, I've been trying to hide how much I miss him, and suddenly, all the agony of the situation hits me. My heart aches to hear the sound of his voice again, or even to see a text message from him.

WE MET BACK in middle school when he joined my class quite early into the year. He was a transfer student from Sweden and didn't know English very well. Since I was one of the more outgoing students, he was placed under my care, and we quickly became friends. I think that's when I started to fall in love with him but didn't realize it since I was so young.

I remember being incredibly fond of him, feelings that I didn't quite understand back then, but they're clear to me now.

We spent every break we had together, just talking about random things, making daisy chains on the field during the summer. I can vividly remember the way his eyes lit up when I placed one that I'd made onto his beautiful blonde hair.

I enjoyed middle school. We'd spent so much time together after school and during. I had lots of other friends apart from him, but he became my favorite quickly after we had first met. I tried to introduce him to my other friends, but they never really got along very well since he didn't understand them.

So, we spent most of our time alone. I tried my best to teach him my language as best I could. Surprisingly, he learned very quickly and could speak clearly to me in no time. The first time he ever made my heart, really beat, was when he pulled me into a big hug, letting me rest my head on his as we embraced. I was taller than him at the time, but he quickly grew to be much bigger than me. We stayed in that hug for a while. I still don't really know why he decided to do it. Maybe he just wasn't feeling well that day.

AFTER SEEING THAT PICTURE, I become curious. I want to see more of him. To reminisce on the old times that we had. Swallowing, I click on the photo icon. My eyes are suddenly flooded with pictures of us. Me and my best friend. The best friend whom I was in love with. Whom I'm still in love with.

One of the pictures stick out to me, and I press on it to get a closer look. It's a picture of us both sleeping, taken by another one of our friends at the time.

Back in high school, we had a sleepover at one of our friend's house with a few other people while her parents were out of town. We shared the couch downstairs, and I comfortably rested in his arms the whole night. That's when we shared our first kiss, too, during a classic game of spin the bottle.

Looking back on it now, I can see why our friends tried their hardest to get us together. Despite their efforts though, and my own love for him, he never felt the same way. We took so many pictures that I barely know where to look.

I then scroll back to when we were in high school, when we had taken the most pictures and spent the most time together. There is a group photo with us and all of our high school friends, sitting on the track field for our last day of school picture. Unsurprisingly, Felix and I were cuddled together in the corner of the picture, with some of our friends looking at us fondly.

Chapter Two

I didn't enjoy high school as much as I'd expected to. The days dragged, and I struggled to make a lot of friends. I only had a couple, whom I'd only really met because Felix had made friends with them first. They were a couple of girls, which we grew incredibly close with over time. But still, we were never as close as I was with Felix.

Felix always stayed by my side, defending me from anyone who tried to pick a fight with me. I didn't really have that many arguments with people. I was quieter and tended to keep to myself. But there was one girl who didn't like me at all. I don't personally remember doing anything to annoy her; she had just seemingly taken a disliking to me for no reason. She would pull my hair and shout insults at me.

Now, thinking back, maybe she was jealous; what other reason could there have been? But it made me feel terrible. At first, it didn't bother me that much; I was able to ignore it. But it soon became worse and worse when her friends sometimes joined in.

But she would never say anything to me when Felix was

around, so I'd purposely keep to his side as much as possible to avoid her.

One day though, he finally noticed what was going on when she shouted something at me without realizing that he was nearby. I will always remember how his face twisted into a glare when he realized what she had said. I'd never seen him that angry before. Well, I'd never seen him angry, period. He was always happy, so optimistic.

It resulted in him snapping at her, and she broke down in front of everyone. She was the typical high school bully, so a couple of people chuckled, causing her to get even more upset. The girl never said anything to me again after that, but she always looked like she was carrying a hateful word on her shoulder. Not that I cared much.

One of her friends actually came up to me after that, apologizing for how she had treated me. She told me how much she hated the way they treated people and asked if we could become friends. Of course, I said yes, eager to invite her into my circle. We became very close friends after that, and she actually attended my wedding.

Everything that I had gone through with my parents and other people had convinced me that I didn't deserve his affection, but he always assured me that it was sort of a "thank you" for helping him learn English, and being one of the only people who truly bothered to befriend him. Even though high school wasn't a very memorable experience for me, I do remember being extremely happy with my life. At least, in comparison to how my life actually turned out.

Sure, I love my husband very much, and now that we're married, I wouldn't want to change him for the world. But I still feel robbed of my chance with Felix, even after all this time away from him. I'm still curious about what he could possibly be doing with his life right now.

I continue to flick through the gallery. The way his eyes

look at me so lovingly in all of the photos makes me question his feelings, too… But maybe, I was just being hopeful; it's too late now, anyway. Another one of the photos show us eating ice cream together, with some cringey stickers and filters all over the screen.

We were in high school; who could blame us?

Back then, my parents weren't the best, and I had problems with them all the time. We had tons of arguments, which ultimately ended in me getting kicked out of their home constantly. Felix gave me a place to stay, meaning, we spent most of our time together. Ultimately, my feelings for him became stronger, and I became more and more attached to him.

Even though my home life was bad, Felix and his parents made it a lot better. I felt comfortable at his house and was allowed to stay whenever I needed to. My parents were going through a pretty rough divorce, and I seemingly "got in the way" — their words — so Felix gave me a place to stay while they recovered and regained their time for me.

The time we spent at his house wasn't very eventful. He still only saw me as his best friend, so the most we ever did was cuddle and watch endless amounts of movies. But it was enough to make me extremely happy at the time. I would lay my head on his chest and listen to the sound of his heart beating peacefully. His hand would wrap around my waist and pull me closer to him. We would also sleep like that, too, his arms around me and my arms around him.

Back then, I was convinced that he would be able to hear the sound of my heartbeat from where he lied. It was beating so loudly from the experience, and I could only hope that he didn't realize how nervous I was.

I CLUTCH onto the cabinets as I feel my knees weaken. My head feels so hot, and my heart is throbbing. Why is this happening? Part of me wishes that my husband had left the phone in the attic, along with everything I still feel for Felix. But another part of me is grateful.

To this day, I still miss him. In the end, I never even got a chance to say goodbye to him. It was so strange, the way we could go from being best friends to being strangers within minutes.

The sound of my son crying suddenly distracts me from my thoughts. I place the phone down on the counter so it can charge, and I go to check on him.

"Are you hungry?" I ask as I pick him up from the ground, taking him to the kitchen for breakfast.

I place him in his highchair and pour out a bowl of cereal and milk. As I go to give it to him, I notice something. His blonde hair looks just like Felix's, and the loving look in his eyes as he stare at me is also the same.

I must've been staring for a short while, because he starts to speak. "Mommy?"

"Sorry." I shake the thought from my head and place the bowl on the highchair, along with a plastic spoon for him to eat with.

Now, everything I look at reminds me of him. Even the countertops remind me of when we would bake cookies together, and he'd lift me up to sit on top of it like a child. He always said that it was to get me out of the way. Thinking back on it now, it makes me chuckle. I can finally see why our friends thought we had something.

My son finishes up with his meal, and I let him out of the chair, placing the bowl into the sink to be washed later. Now that the children are busy, I have another chance to look through the phone. Picking it up once again, I open my messages, desperate to look at what we used to talk about.

When the texts eventually load, I'm able to read the last few ones we ever sent to each other.

LAUREN

> I hope I can see you again soon :)
> Goodnight, please sleep well.

FELIX

> We'll meet again soon! I'll only stay here for
> a short while so I can visit my grandparents,
> and then we'll finally be reunited.
> Goodnight, love.

We never spoke again after that. I heard from another friend that he met some girl while he was back home visiting his grandparents, and decided that he was going to stay with her. He felt too guilty to speak to me himself, so he stuck to communicating through our friends, which I hated.

I scroll up a few months, before he went away, to one of my favorite memories. One that I will never be able to forget, no matter how much I try to force myself to. I find what I'm looking for and begin to read through the messages.

FELIX

> I'm sorry about what happened... We were
> both really drunk, and I guess what
> happened, happened. Let's just forget
> about it, okay?

The first time we went out to drink as legal adults ended in us getting carried away and spending the night together. Secretly, I wanted us to pursue what happened further, and finally make things official, but I could've never said that to him. Before all of that happened, however, I did make an attempt to tell him my feelings, but it didn't go how I had expected, and he shrugged me off.

I find the chat, exhaling loudly as I remember the pain I felt back then.

LAUREN

Do you really love me, Felix? I love you so much that it hurts, and I can't keep acting like I don't.

FELIX

Of course, I do. You're my best friend, after all :) Did something happen?

LAUREN

No, my day just hasn't been great. I'm going to sleep now.

FELIX

Sleep well. I'll see you in the morning.

After that experience, it was clear to me that he didn't want anything more than what we already had. I felt so stupid that seeing him every day after that just felt embarrassing, and he still has no idea how I feel.

Or maybe he does, and just chooses to ignore it.

Chapter Three

We didn't have many classes together in college. I only saw him when our breaks lined up. And we tried our best to see each other as much as we could. However, he became pretty popular in college, with girls constantly trying to get with him. Of course, this made me extremely jealous, and I subtly tried to make it seem like he already had a girlfriend so they'd leave him alone.

I'd give him my hair ties and bracelets to wear on his wrists. Rings for his fingers. "Accidentally" spray him with my perfume. But nothing really fully kept everyone away from him, and he didn't wear them often. I wonder if he still has them?

There was this one girl who was totally infatuated with him, and she constantly messaged him and tried to hang out with us. Every time I saw her, I acted extra clingy around him, holding onto his arms, hugging him. It got to the point where she asked me herself if we were dating, since she wanted to ask him out. I absent-mindedly told her that we were so she wouldn't make an attempt at getting together with him.

The next day, he asked me why I told her that we were

dating. That's when I broke down. I remember crying more than I ever had before, and telling him that I was terrified of being replaced with someone else. He told me he didn't like her anyway, and she left us alone.

Along with everything else that happened in college, we stayed great friends. I managed to make a few new friends of my own, but Felix never really spoke that often with them since I wanted to keep him all for myself. It sounds selfish now, but at the time, I was so in love with him that I didn't care. I don't think I remember arguing with him once the whole time we were friends. After everything we had been through, I was convinced that he was my soulmate. And that if I was patient enough, everything would fall into place, and we could spend our lives together.

At least, I was hopeful back then. I don't think I would've made it through the long days without crying, otherwise. The way my heart yearned for him to become mine made me feel awful. But the things he did would make me happier than ever. So, I couldn't get enough of him and his presence.

Once college was over, we each got different jobs and agreed that when we earned enough money, we would buy a house and move in together. I remember him explaining to me how he wanted his wedding to be, what he wanted his kids to be like. As much as I wanted to ask him to share his life with me, I didn't, and instead, spoke about my own ideas for a wedding, which were pretty similar to his. I saved up a lot of money for our house, and that was when he told me he was going back to Sweden to see his family. The news that broke my heart.

But we made a promise to see each other again soon, and then we would be able to move in together and start building a life together as best friends.

But that day never came. The stories I heard about him were all different. I never did see him again. However, if the story about him meeting another girl back home was true, I hope she treats him well. I hope she loves him as much as I have loved him during all these years.

After I heard that news, I cried for weeks. My mind couldn't think about anyone else but the man whom I've pursued my whole life, falling in love with someone else. I went into the dating game, trying everything I could to forget about him, burying away the memories that we created together. I threw my phone away and started anew, vowing to never think about or contact him again. As much as it killed me, I needed to do it for my own happiness.

I met Clarke, my husband, during that time, too. I loved him, obviously. But as guilty as I am to say this, I don't think I love him as much as I'd loved, and still love, Felix. I don't think I could ever love anyone as much as I love him. I don't want to say that I regret my marriage to my husband, but the feeling dawns on me.

Despite this, I have no way of ever contacting Felix again, so moving on is my only hope at living a normal life.

I TURN the phone off and place it to one side of the counter, feeling dizzy from the overwhelming number of emotions currently residing in my body. I crave seeing other things that I can remember him by, anything other than this phone. Things that are much more personal.

Gulping, I make my way toward the attic. I had kept some things up there when he left, even though I tried to convince myself to get rid of them so I could forget. I couldn't bring myself to do it and kept everything instead in a big box, which I hid in the attic.

I pull down the ladder and start to climb up, watching my step on the way up. I'm not as agile as I used to be.

Once I'm up, I turn on the lightbulb and look around, silently praying that Clarke hadn't meddled in my old boxes and thrown them away. Fortunately, my eyes land upon a carboard box, which has the word "memories" sprawled across the side of it in black sharpie ink. That's exactly what I'm looking for.

Moving some of the other things out of the way, I pull the box toward me, sitting down beside it and pulling open the lid, immediately greeted with an old, familiar scent.

The first thing I lay my hand on is an old diary. I remember that I had written about him a lot in here during high school. I open the first page, listening to the crackle of the spine as I do so. Seeing my old handwriting on the page really takes me back. It's surprising how much handwriting can change over time.

I take a moment to read through the diary, remembering all of the events that happened in there as clear as day.

December 11, 2001

Today was boring. I saw Felix a lot, though! Our class was cancelled, so we ended up sitting outside the classroom and sharing a snack while we waited for the day to end. It was a new type of food from his home country. I can't remember the name, though; it was something complicated.

December 12, 2001

It's finally Friday! Felix invited me to stay over at his house during the weekend since my parents are arguing again (no surprise there).

But I'm happy that we can spend time together; he makes me so happy. I'm glad we're friends. Tonight, we're going to bake cookies and watch lots of movies.

December 14, 2001

I couldn't write over the weekend since I wasn't at home, but I had a great time at Felix's! We watched so many movies, and his parents are great cooks. I ate so much good food that I felt like my stomach was going to explode.

I took a shower at his house and used some of his shampoo, so my hair smells just like him now. I don't think I'll be washing it for a while. I'm wearing his clothes, too. They're kind of baggy on me. It's weird that I used to be so much bigger than him at the start of high school.

Last night, his parents asked us if we think we'll be friends forever. And Felix said yes! That made me smile. Although, I hope that we can become something more than just friends soon... Maybe we can date?

December 15, 2001

I hate Mondays. We have this really awful teacher who hates me for no reason at all. Every

time I try to speak to him, he ignores me. He
adores Felix, though. I wonder what it's like to
be liked by absolutely everyone… Felix and I
made a daisy chain during lunch, though, so
that was nice. We got carried away, and it
ended up being really long!

I skip through a few pages in the diary, trying to find
something interesting inside. I then come across a particular
page that's covered in smudged ink and wet stains, hinting that
I had indeed been crying on this page.

January 10, 2002

I love Felix so much. But he will never know
that because I'm too scared to tell him. I'm
terrified of losing him, and it seems like no
matter what I do, he will drift away from me.
I wish I knew how to keep him to myself
forever. Every time I think about him, my heart
aches. I feel so stupid; how could I have
fallen this deeply in love with my best friend?
I haven't slept properly in days because I'm
terrified of him replacing me with somebody
else.

January 11, 2002

I feel much better today. I spoke to Felix
about my feelings a little… He assured me that

he won't ever replace me with anyone else, and I'll always be his bestest friend. Still, I haven't confessed my feelings to him yet. I don't think I ever will, only in my dreams. I had a good dream last night. I got married to Felix, we had two children, and were happy and in love. I'd like to think that's our future, and I'm some sort of fortune teller. We are soulmates, after all.

January 12, 2002

Today was so scary. Felix almost read my diary! I invited him over to my house for a while, which is rare because my parents never let us see each other. But they're out of town right now. Anyway, I asked him to grab something for me out of my bedside drawer. That is the drawer in which I keep this diary! I'm so dumb; I should have thought about that before asking him. He picked it up and asked, "What's this?" And opened the first page! I had to grab it away from him quickly and say that I wrote about some private stuff in there that he wouldn't want to know about. That could've been so embarrassing...

January 13, 2002

Felix ended up staying the night since it started to rain, and I didn't want him to walk home in the rain. I had to sneak him out in the morning, though. If my parents ever find out I had a boy in the house overnight, I'm certain that they'll kill me.

Oh, well, at least last night was fun. We talked about some fun stuff, about what type of wedding we want! And baby names. I'm not sure if I'd want any children in the future; they seem like a pain. But if they were with Felix, it would be okay, I think. Everyone loves Felix! I don't know whether I'm happy about that or not...

Closing the diary, I rummage through the box, certain that I had kept the daisy chain that we made during that one lunch. The memories are all flowing back to me now. I can remember everything that we did together, and it makes me sad. But reminiscing on the past is good sometimes, I think. It helps you to appreciate it more. I finally find the daisy chain and pull it out of the box.

The daisy chain is completely squashed from being in that box for such a long time. Plus, the flowers are dead (which is no surprise), but I can still remember when we made it. He would pass me the daisies he had picked from the grass bank. Our fingers would touch for a moment while I took it from him, and I would add it to our chain. We ended up doing that during most of our break, so it got pretty long.

I gently place the daisy chain down on the ground. I definitely should have found a way to preserve it better. But it doesn't matter now. I dig my hand into the box and pull out a piece of paper. It's thick and crumpled, with some of the ink smudged down the page. Looking at the drawing, I can tell that it was a drawing of me. Short, straight blonde hair, brown eyes. It's a picture that Felix had drawn of me while I was sleeping at his house.

He had always enjoyed art, and sketched a lot even in middle school. In this picture, I was wrapped up in his blankets, my mouth slightly agape as I did so. At the time, I almost cried when he showed it to me and told me to keep it. But I kept my cool.

Chuckling at the memory, I place it down and reach my hand into the box to try and find something else.

My hand lands on a small jewelry box, and I can immediately tell what it is. I flick open the velvet lid to reveal a silver necklace. My birthday present. When Felix had given it to me, he told me to close my eyes and hold up my hair, to which I did. And then he wrapped it around my neck, clipping it gently around me. There was a locket attached to it, which contained a picture of us both. The gift meant the world to me, and I wore it everywhere. Only stopping when I heard about him meeting somebody new.

As much as I love Felix, he confuses me. I thought that we were something more than just friends, always. The way he treated me signaled that we were something more. The hugs he gave me weren't just friendly. Our first times for everything were with each other. I rejected every boy who tried to make a move on me, all because I thought I would have a chance with him.

Chapter Four

To this day, I still blame myself for that. I still think that my confession could've been better, or I should have messaged him more when he was away to prevent us from drifting apart like we did. I couldn't even do anything to stop us from drifting, but instead, I just sat and cried.

Letting out a sigh, I place the jewelry box on the ground beside the diary and daisy chain. Something else in the box catches my eye. It's a little pink dinosaur plushie. Like the ones that you win at the fair. Felix had one, too, but his was blue. We both decided to name them after each other, and promised to keep them forever. I do still wonder if he kept that promise. I'm sure he did.

I hold the plushie in my hand, squeezing it a little, and it still feels soft. Even though it had been in my attic all this time. As for how we got them, we actually won them at a fair. Well, Felix did. It was a game of basketball. Dunk one, and get a prize. Of course, Felix won. He was seemingly good at everything, after all. He won one for me, and one for himself. That was also when we promised to keep them forever.

During our time at the fair, we tried to ride everything. Just to get our money's worth. It was fun, though. I spent my time clinging onto Felix's hands on the bigger rides. Not because I was scared, but because I wanted some kind of excuse to hold him. His hands felt so warm in the freezing cold weather.

I pull out something else, something that, even now, makes me blush. It's a pregnancy test, and it's positive. But it had turned out to be wrong once we got to the hospital.

When Felix and I spent that night together, we didn't bother to use any kind of protection since we were both too drunk to even comprehend the situation. But I can still remember the passionate way he kissed me. I should've known then that he loved me like I loved him. No one kisses their best friend that way.

Now, it seems strange to save something like this, but I never want to forget that time we spent together. I thought that I would've been relieved when the doctors told me that I was certainly not pregnant. But instead, I felt a little disappointed. I wouldn't have been opposed to having a child with him. But even if I were truly pregnant, I wouldn't have known what to do.

It was hard when I had my first child with Clarke. It would've been unimaginable if I'd had a child when I was that young. I remember Felix being terrified, more scared than I was. Maybe because he didn't want a child when we were still in college. It was understandable, after all.

Everything that had happened between us back then didn't matter anymore. Our childhood was over, just like the tight bond that we had shared. I knew that nothing was bound to last forever, but I was convinced that we would be the ones who did.

I start to place everything I had pulled out back into the

box, taking one last look at the memories I was putting away. This time, hopefully, forever.

I hear the front door open and rush back down the stairs, returning the ladder to its natural state. I can't have Clarke knowing about my feelings for my best friend. I feel a tear run down my right cheek as I hear him greet our children. I feel so guilty for regretting my marriage with him…

If I had confessed to Felix properly, would things be different now? Quickly, I wipe away my tears and try to ignore the aching feeling inside my heart. Time had flown by while I was thinking about my old life with Felix, and before I knew it, it's time to face my husband. The marriage that I am now finding myself regretting after all these years.

In fact, despite my feelings now, I did have the picture-perfect wedding that I had described to Felix, just without him. I had the perfect children that I had once described to Felix, just not with him like I had always hoped. I'm aware that I'd made some mistakes along the way during my lifetime. I only wish that I had at least stayed in contact with him, even if we just stayed friends. I crave his presence again, and I want to know if he's doing okay.

"Honey, did you have a good day?" Clarke smiles at me when our eyes meet, his hands placing themselves on my waist.

"Yeah, it was okay."

His eyes then land on the phone behind me. "Did you look through the phone?"

I nod. "I looked through it. There's nothing important on there. You can get rid of it, only old high school memories that I'd like to forget."

All the pictures with him, the messages, everything, will die, along with this phone.

"Alright, then. I'll get rid of it." He picks the phone up off the kitchen counter and click the on button. "I'll have to restore it to its factory settings first. Meaning that everything on here will be unrecoverable... Is there anything you'd like to take off here first?"

I shake my head. "It's all just old junk that I don't need anymore."

"What's the password?"

I take the phone from his hand and type in the password, looking at the picture of me and Felix one more time before giving it back to him.

"Thank you..." He looks at the phone for a moment. "I was thinking. You've never mentioned a guy like this before. Was he your old boyfriend or something?"

I let out a sad chuckle. "No, he was just my friend..."

I try to hold back more tears... My boyfriend? My soulmate? My best friend? I have no idea. I'm still confused, even after all this time... Pathetic.

"Then I'll go ahead and delete everything, and we can go sell it in the morning. We might even be able to get some money back."

He gives me a smile, and I watch as he clicks the factory reset button. My heart is pounding in my chest. Am I making the right decision here?

My husband places the phone in his pocket and goes to check on the children, leaving me in the kitchen with my thoughts.

I'd like to think that my friendship with Felix never ended. We never argued, simply just drifted. And if we ever meet again, which is very unlikely... we will become good friends again.

It's too late to pursue a relationship now. But I'll be happy just to see his face again.

There's one last thing I need to do before my past can be fully erased... I follow my husband into the living room to see him holding our son.

"Honey... I checked the attic earlier, and there are some

boxes that I need to get rid of. Will you help me carry them to the car?"

All that's left is to erase my high school self. The diary, the daisy chain, the drawing, the necklace, the plushie. I will never truly be free unless they are all gone, too. I feel my heart break a little when I see my husband turn his head and give me a small nod.

"Show me what I'm bringing down, and we'll take it right away. The kids can come, too. It will be good for them to get some fresh air."

We both head up to the attic. The whole way there, I question my decision, but it's something I know I need to do. To kill off the memories that have been stopping me from living my life this whole time. I point to the box that I had been looking at earlier. The box full of my memories.

My husband crouches down beside the box, reading the text written along the side of it. "Memories? Are you sure that you want to get rid of this?"

He tries to open the box to look inside, but I stop him. I can't show him my past. I won't! What will he think of me if he finds out that I'm still hung up on my childhood best friend?

My hand grips onto his, stopping him from looking inside. "Yeah. There's nothing really in there. Nothing that I need. It's just junk. You've saved a lot of trash from when you were young. I'm sure you know what I mean." I give him a small, fake smile.

Choosing not to question me anymore, he picks up the box and places it under his arm. "Anything else?"

"No. That's it. Will you give me a moment? I need to check some things, and then I'll meet you at the car."

He nods and carefully heads down. I hear him call the kids' names for a brief moment before it goes completely silent. I collapse onto the attic floor, my eyes filling up with tears. My body aches, and my head feels like it could explode any minute. Why does it have to end like this? I was so happy with him.

"Why did you leave me?!" I scream out, my hands clutching tightly at my shirt.

I let the tears flow down my face, the tears that I had worked so hard to keep in all this time. I even wanted to cry on my own wedding day, and when my children were born. All because I felt like I was with the wrong person. I'm still so attached to Felix, even though he's thousands of miles away now, impossible to find.

I take a minute to clean myself up. I need to face the present now and stop dwelling on the past. Felix is gone, along with all of our memories. After everything we had gone through, I hope Felix is living a happy, fulfilling life. And I hope that he still thinks about me and the life we shared from time to time. But no matter how much I want to forget about him and move on with my own life, just like he has, I can't help but feel desperate to tell him the words "I love you" one more time.

And this time, it will be for real...

I rub my eyes and climb down the ladder. There is just one thing that I want to take out of the box. Now that my decision on what I will do next is final, I want to take one thing with me. I open the trunk of the car and search through the box until I find the jewelry box. Taking out the necklace, I look at the picture in the locket one last time.

Felix knew that this picture is my favorite of us. It shows the both of us in his parents' car, heading to the beach. We were both smiling and eating ice cream. That was one of those times when I was truly happy. I close the locket and clasp it around my neck, not having Felix to help me do it this time. I adjust it, and then go to sit in the passenger seat of the car, beside my husband.

"Are you ready? You sure you want to throw that stuff out?" His eyes wander to the necklace that I am now wearing, and I quickly cover it with my hand.

"I'm ready... Let's go." I want to get this over with as quickly as possible.

My heart already aches, and I can't wait for it to stop for good.

The drive to the dumping site is becoming one of the longest drives of my life. The car is almost completely silent, the quiet sound of the radio the only thing keeping me from going completely insane. My heart is beating out of my chest, and I can feel it against my fingers as I hold onto the locket.

I stare out the window the whole time, passing by all of the happy families. I feel terrible. I had ruined our perfect relationship with my stupid feelings. Otherwise, we would be just like those happy couples.

Finally, we arrive at the site. Clarke tries to get out of the car, but I stop him.

"Let me take it; I'll be alright."

Without waiting for him to respond, I climb out of the car, slamming the door behind me, and headed toward the trunk. Opening it up, my eyes glance at the box. "Memories" was still written on the side. I grab the box and carry it toward one of the garbage bins, my hands clutching tightly against the cardboard. Now that I'm actually doing it, it feels wrong. But this is the only way.

Without dwelling on it any further, I heave the box toward the bin, watching as it gets lost in the heaps and mounds of cardboard. You can barely even tell them apart now, my whole childhood mixed with a bunch of old, dirty cardboard boxes. Not turning back, I head back to the car, my husband looking at me worriedly the whole way.

Once I sit back down, my husband places his hand on my knee gently. "Are you okay? You look upset, and your eyes are all puffy and red..." He pauses for a moment to look outside at the dumping site. "What did you throw away?"

"I told you; it's just a box." I turn to face him, and our eyes meet for a moment.

I quickly turn away from him again. The pain is too unbearable. I can't even love my own husband anymore, not after everything I had remembered today.

"Do you want to talk about it?" His hand leaves my knee and caresses the locket on my necklace.

I shake my head and quickly pull away from him. "I'm going to walk home. I need some time alone. Besides, it's not a long walk." I push open the car door, hesitating for a second before turning back to give my husband a kiss on the cheek.

"Do you want to take the kids with you? For company?"

"Take them home. I have some things I need to take care of before I head back."

I stretch over to the back seat to cover my children in kisses before I leave. It will be my last chance, after all.

I climb out of the car and wave goodbye to them, a single tear falling down my face. As I clutch onto the locket and walk, I think about how selfish I'm being. Choosing to leave a caring husband and beautiful children behind, all for someone I no longer even associate with. But the pain is so bad; I want it all to be over.

Walking in the opposite direction of my home, I stare upwards at the clouds, trying to make shapes out of them. Just like I used to do with Felix. In fact, I can almost hear him say, "Look! A sheep!"

Today, I will make sure that those memories die alongside me. I can't face anything anymore. I have become way too reliant on someone who is completely out of my reach. Someone who has moved on from me and our life together.

When today is over, I hope that I can be reborn. And I can finally live the life I had hoped for with Felix. Maybe this time around, it will be perfect. The perfect wedding, beautiful children we pick out baby names together for.

And if I'm not reborn with Felix, I'll do this over and over, an endless cycle to ensure our happiness. If I get the opportunity to do all of this again, to relive my time with Felix, I will do it right. I will do everything in my power to make him stay.

I will stay by his side forever.

The End

Stalk the Author

Website:

https://www.kathrynreign.com/

Facebook Page:

https://www.facebook.com/authorkathrynreign

Instagram:

https://www.instagram.com/authorkathrynreign/

Goodreads:

https://www.goodreads.com/author/show/21854875.
Kathryn_Reign

BookBub:

https://www.bookbub.com/authors/kathryn-reign

In Love with my Best Friend